CORAL ISLAND

BY R. M. BALLANTYNE

Retold by Derek Lord

Illustrated by John Cooper

PURNELL
London, W.1.

It was a wild night of howling storm when I was born on the foaming bosom of the broad Atlantic Ocean. My father was a sea-captain and, as far back as our family could be traced, it had been connected with the great watery waste.

Thus it was, I suppose, that I came to inherit a roving disposition and, as soon as I was old enough, went to sea as an apprentice on a coasting vessel.

My Christian name was Ralph, and my companions soon added Rover to it when they learnt how much I wished to travel to every part of the world.

Of all the places which the older seamen described, the Coral Islands of the South Pacific captured my imagination most and, when I reached the age of fifteen, I resolved to make a voyage there.

My father placed me under the charge of an old messmate of his, a merchant captain, who was about to sail his fine ship, the *Arrow*, on a trading mission to the Pacific islands.

It was a bright, beautiful, warm day when our ship spread her canvas to the breeze, and my heart bounded with delight as I listened to the merry chorus of the sailors while they hauled at the ropes and raised the anchor.

There were a number of boys in the ship, but two of them were my special favourites. Jack Martin was a tall, strapping, broad-shouldered youth of eighteen, with a handsome, good-humoured, firm face. He had had a good education, was clever

and hearty and lion-like in his actions, but mild and quiet in disposition. My other companion was Peterkin Gay. He was little, quick, funny, mischievous, and about fourteen years old.

When we approached Cape Horn, at the southern tip of South America, the weather became cold and stormy, and the sailors began to tell stories about the furious gales and danger of that terrible cape. Nevertheless, we passed round it and entered the Pacific Ocean without much rough weather, and sailed on before a warm, tropical breeze until we reached the coral islands.

One night, an awful storm burst upon the *Arrow*. The first squall of wind carried away two of our masts, and left only the foremast standing. For five days the tempest raged, and everything was swept off the decks except one small boat. The captain said that he had no idea where we were, and all of us feared that we might get among the dangerous coral reefs which are so numerous in the Pacific.

At daybreak on the sixth morning of the gale, we saw land ahead. It was an island, encircled by a reef of coral on which the

waves broke in a fury. There was calm water within this reef, but we could see only one narrow opening into it. For this opening we steered; but, before the ship reached it, a tremendous wave broke on our stern, tore the rudder completely off, and left us at the mercy of the winds and waves.

"It's all over with us now, lads!" said the captain to the men. "Get the boat ready to launch."

"Come, boys," said Jack Martin, in a grave tone, to me and Peterkin, as we stood on the quarter-deck awaiting our fate — "we three shall stick together. The little boat will be sure to upset, so I mean rather to trust myself to a large oar. I see through the telescope that the ship will strike at the tail of the reef, where the waves break into the quiet water inside; so, if we manage to cling to the oar till it is driven over the breakers, we may perhaps gain the shore. What say you, will you join me?"

We gladly agreed to follow Jack, for he inspired us with confidence, although I could perceive, by the sad tone of his voice, that he had little hope.

The ship was now very near the rocks. The men were ready with the boat, the captain beside them giving orders, when a tremendous wave came towards us. We three ran towards the bow to lay hold of our oar, and had barely reached it when the wave fell on the deck with a crash like thunder. At the same moment the ship struck, the foremast broke off close to the deck and went over the side, carrying the boat and men with it. Our oar got entangled with the wreck, and Jack seized an axe to cut it free; but owing to the motion of the ship, he missed the cordage, and struck the axe deep into the oar. Another wave, however, washed it clear of the wreck. We all seized hold of it, and the next instant we were struggling in the wild sea. The last thing I saw was the boat whirling in the surf and then I became insensible.

10

On recovering from my swoon, I found myself lying on a bank of soft grass, under shelter of an overhanging rock, with Peterkin on his knees by my side, tenderly bathing my temples with water, and endeavouring to stop the blood that flowed from a wound in my forehead.

"Speak to us, my dear Ralph," whispered Jack. "Are you better now?"

I smiled and looked up, saying, "Better! Why, what do you mean, Jack? I'm quite well."

"Then what are you shamming for, and frightening us in this way?" said Peterkin.

I now raised myself on my elbow, and putting my hand to my forehead, found that it had been cut pretty severely, and that I had lost a good deal of blood.

"The captain and crew, what of them, Jack?" I inquired anxiously.

"After we landed, I saw them hoist some sort of sail—a blanket, I fancy, for it was too small for the boat—and in half an hour they were out of sight."

"What has become of the wreck, Jack?" asked Peterkin. "I saw you clambering up the rocks there while I was watching Ralph. Did you say she had gone to pieces?"

"No, she has not gone to pieces, but she has gone to the bottom," replied Jack. "So, if this is a desert island, we shall have to live very much like the wild beasts, for we have not a tool of any kind, not even a knife."

"Yes, we have that," said Peterkin, fumbling in his trousers pocket, from which he drew forth a small penknife, with only one blade, and that was broken.

"Well, that's better than nothing. But come," said Jack, rising, "we are wasting our time in talking instead of doing. You seem well enough to walk now, Ralph. Let us see what we have got in our pockets, and then let us climb some hill and ascertain what sort of island we have been cast upon, for, whether good or bad, it seems likely to be our home for some time to come."

We seated ourselves upon a rock, and began to look over our personal property. When all was collected together, we found that our worldly goods consisted of the following articles: first, a small penknife with a single blade broken off about the middle and very rusty, besides having two or three notches on its edge; second, a pencil-case without any lead in it; third, a piece of whip-cord about six yards long; fourth, a sail-maker's needle of a small size; fifth, a ship's telescope, the glass at the small end of which was broken to pieces; our sixth article was a brass ring which Jack always wore on his little finger. In addition to these articles we had a little bit of tinder, and the clothes on our backs.

While we were examining these things and talking about them, Jack suddenly started and exclaimed:

"The oar! We have forgotten the oar—there's a bit of hoop iron at the end of it that may be of use to us."

As we hastened down to the beach, I looked well about me

and realized that the gale had died away. A sandy beach of dazzling whiteness lined our hilly island's bright-green shore, and upon it there fell a gentle ripple of the sea. About a mile distant from the shore, I saw the great billows of the ocean rolling like a green wall, and falling with a loud roar upon a low coral reef, where they were dashed into white foam and flung up in clouds of spray. We afterwards found that this coral reef extended quite round the island, and thus formed a natural breakwater to it so that, between the reef and the shore, the sea was calm and smooth.

"Here it is, boys, hurrah! Come on! Just what we want," cried Peterkin, who had reached the water's edge ahead of us and was tugging at something with all his power.

On coming up we found that Peterkin was vainly trying to pull the axe out of the oar, into which, it will be remembered, Jack struck it while endeavouring to cut away the cordage among which it had become entangled at the bow of the ship. Fortunately for us the axe had remained fast in the oar, and even now all Peterkin's strength could not draw it out of the cut.

"Ah! That is capital indeed!" cried Jack, at the same time giving the axe a wrench that plucked it out of the tough wood. "And what is more, there is a useful piece of hoop iron nailed round the blade of the oar to prevent it from splitting."

On our way back from the shore, it suddenly came into Peterkin's head that we had nothing to eat except the wild berries which grew in profusion almost everywhere.

"What shall we do, Jack?" said he, with a rueful look. "Perhaps they may be poisonous!"

"No fear!" replied Jack. "I have observed that a few of them are not unlike some of the berries that grow wild on our hills at home. But look up there, Peterkin," continued Jack, pointing to a coconut-palm. "There are nuts for us in all stages."

"So there are!" cried Peterkin, who immediately bounded up the tall stem of the tree like a squirrel and returned with three nuts, each as large as a fist.

It was beginning to grow dark when we returned to our encampment, so we put off our visit to the top of a hill till next day, and employed the light that yet remained to us in cutting down a quantity of boughs and the broad leaves of a tree. With these we erected a sort of rustic bower, in which we meant to pass the night. There was no absolute necessity for this, because the air of our island was so genial and balmy that we could have slept quite well without any shelter, but we were so little used to sleeping in the open air, that we did not quite relish the idea of lying down without any covering over us; besides, our bower would shelter us if it should happen to rain. Having strewed the floor with leaves and dry grass, we bethought ourselves of supper.

But now it occurred to us, for the first time, that we had no means of making a fire.

"Now, there's a fix! What shall we do?" said Peterkin, while we both turned our eyes to Jack, to whom we always looked in our difficulties. Jack seemed rather perplexed.

"There are flints enough, no doubt, on the beach," said he, "but they are of no use at all without a steel."

"I have it!" cried Peterkin. "The spy-glass—the big glass at the end is a burning-glass!"

"You forget that we have no sun," said I.

"Ah, boys, I've got it now!" exclaimed Jack, rising and cutting a branch from a neighbouring bush, which he stripped of its leaves. "I recollect seeing this done once at home. Hand me the bit of whip-cord." With the cord and branch, Jack soon formed a bow. Then he cut a piece, about three inches long, off the end of a dead branch, which he pointed at the two ends. Round this he passed the cord of the bow, and placed one end against his chest, which was protected from its point by a chip of wood; the other point he placed against the bit of tinder, and then began to saw vigorously with the bow. In a few seconds, the tinder began to smoke; in less than a minute, it caught fire; and in less than a quarter of an hour, we were drinking coconut milk, and eating the nuts themselves, round a fire that would have roasted an entire sheep, while the smoke, flames and sparks flew up among the broad leaves of the over-hanging palm trees, and cast a warm glow upon our leafy bower.

18

That night the starry sky looked down through the gently-rustling trees upon our slumbers, and the distant roaring of the surf upon the coral reef was our lullaby.

What a joyful thing it is to awaken, on a fresh, glorious morning, and find the rising sun staring into your face with dazzling brilliancy. How wonderful, too, to have the sea on your doorstep, inviting you to take a dip before breakfast. That first morning on Coral Island, we needed no persuasion at all. While Peterkin enjoyed himself in the shallow water and in running along the beach, Jack and I swam out into the deep water, and occasionally dived for stones. I shall never forget my delight on first beholding the bottom of the sea within the reef. The bottom of the lagoon was covered with coral of every shape, size and colour, and among this there grew large quantities of seaweed of the richest hues imaginable, and of the most graceful forms; while innumerable fishes —blue, red, yellow, green and striped—sported in and out amongst the flower-beds of this submarine garden.

Jack made a number of dives to collect oysters. "Breakfast enough here," said he, holding them aloft as we landed and ran up the beach. "Hullo, Peterkin! Here you are, boy — split open these fellows while Ralph and I put on our clothes. They'll agree with the coconuts excellently, I have no doubt."

Peterkin, who was already dressed, took the oysters, and opened them with the edge of our axe, exclaiming, "Now that is capital! There's nothing I'm so fond of."

We had no difficulty with the fire that morning, as our burning-glass was an admirable one; and while we roasted a few oysters and ate our coconuts, we held a long conversation about our plans for the day.

We decided to make an excursion to the top of the mountains of the interior, in order to obtain a good view of our island, and first walked a short distance along the beach, till we came to the entrance of a valley through which flowed a rivulet. Here we turned our backs on the sea and struck into the interior, directing our course along the banks of the rivulet towards the foot of a hill, from the top of which a fine view might be obtained.

On reaching the summit, a grand prospect met our gaze.

We found that this was not the highest part of the island, but
that another hill lay beyond, with a wide valley between it
and the one on which we stood. This valley was full of rich
trees, some dark and some light green, some heavy and thick
in foliage, and others light, feathery, and graceful, while the
beautiful blossoms on many of them threw a sort of rainbow
tint over all, and gave to the valley the appearance of a garden
of flowers. Among these we recognized many bread-fruit trees,
laden with the yellow fruit which is so good to eat, and also
a great many coconut-palms. After gazing our fill, we pushed
down the hillside, crossed the valley, and soon began to ascend
the second mountain. It was clothed with trees nearly to the
top, but the summit was bare, and in some places broken.

We found this to be the highest point of the island, and from it we saw our kingdom lying, as it were, like a map around us.

It consisted of two mountains: the one we guessed at five hundred feet; the other, on which we stood, at three thousand. Between these lay the rich, beautiful valley. This valley crossed the island from one end to the other, being high in the middle and sloping on each side towards the sea. The large mountain sloped, on the side farthest from where we had been wrecked, gradually towards the sea; but although, when viewed at a glance, it had thus a regular sloping appearance, a more careful observation showed that it was broken up into a multitude of very small vales, or rather dells and glens, intermingled with little rugged spots and small but abrupt precipices here and there, with rivulets tumbling over their edges and wandering down the slopes in little white streams, sometimes glistening

among the broad leaves of the bread-fruit and coconut trees, or hiding altogether beneath the rich underwood. At the base of this mountain lay a narrow, bright-green plain or meadow, which ended abruptly at the shore. On the other side of the island, whence we had come, stood the smaller hill, at the foot of which diverged three valleys; one being that which we had ascended, with a smaller vale on each side of it, and separated from it by the two ridges before mentioned. In these smaller valleys there were no streams, but they were clothed with the same luxuriant vegetation.

The diameter of the island seemed to be about ten miles, and as it was almost circular in form, its circumference must have been thirty miles. It was belted by a beach of pure white sand, on which lapped the gentle ripples of the lagoon. We now also observed that the coral reef completely encircled the island.

Full of these discoveries, we returned to our encampment, satisfied in our minds that the island was uninhabited.

One morning, whilst bathing, we had a narrow escape from a shark which had entered the lagoon. After that we were forced to bathe in the shallow water, so Jack and I found that the one great source of our enjoyment was gone, for we could no longer dive down among the beautiful coral groves of the sea-bed.

In consequence, we started to search for a large pool among the rocks, where the water would be deep enough for diving, yet so surrounded by rocks as to prevent sharks from getting at us. And such a pool we found. It was situated not more than ten minutes' walk from our camp, and was in the form of a small, deep bay or basin, the entrance to which, besides being narrow, was so shallow that no fish as large as a shark could get in.

Inside the basin, which we called our Water Garden, the

coral formations were much more wonderful, and the sea-weed plants far more lovely and vividly coloured than in the lagoon itself; and the water was so clear and still that, although very deep, you could see the minutest object at the bottom. Besides this, there was a ledge of rock which overhung the basin at its deepest part, from which we could dive pleasantly, and whereon Peterkin could sit and see not only all the wonders I had described to him, but also Jack and me creeping amongst the marine shrubbery at the bottom, like—as he expressed it—"two great, white sea-monsters."

Having now got ourselves into a very comfortable condition, we started to talk of a project which we had long had in mind —namely, to travel entirely round the island. Jack proposed that, before undertaking such an excursion, we should supply ourselves with good defensive arms.

"Besides," said Jack, "it won't do for us to live on coconuts and oysters always. I think a little animal food now and then would be good for us; and as there are many small birds among the trees, some of which are probably very good to eat, I think it would be a capital plan to make bows and arrows, with which we could easily knock them over."

Peterkin and I thought this an excellent plan; but, as evening was fast approaching, Jack needed a good light in which to work. A fire would roast us alive, and we could think of no other means of producing the necessary light until Jack suddenly had a brainwave.

"There is a certain nut growing in these islands," Jack explained, "which is called the candle-nut, because the natives use it instead of candles. I know all about it, and how to prepare it for burning, but I have not seen the tree yet. I believe the nut is about the size of a walnut; and I think that the leaves are white, but I am not sure."

"Eh! Ha! Hum!" exclaimed Peterkin. "I noticed a tree answering to that description this very day."

"Did you?" cried Jack. "Then lead me to it."

In a few minutes, we were all three pushing through the underwood of the forest, headed by Peterkin.

We soon came to the tree in question, which, after Jack had closely examined it, we concluded must be the candle-nut tree. We filled our pockets with nuts, and then Peterkin

swarmed up a coconut-palm to obtain a long branch; from this Jack stripped off a curious substance resembling cloth, which was wrapped round the thick end of the stalk, where it had been cut from the tree. Then, from one of the leaflets on the branch, Jack cut out the central spine or stalk, and hurried back with it to our camp. Having made a small fire, he baked the nuts slightly, and peeled off the husks. After this he wished to bore a hole in them, which, not having anything better at hand at the time, he did with the point of our useless pencil-case. Then he strung them on the coconut spine, and on putting a light to the topmost nut, we found to our great joy that it burned with a clear, beautiful flame.

"Now, lads," said Jack, extinguishing our candle, "the sun

will set in an hour, so we have no time to lose. I shall go out and cut a young tree to make my bow out of, and you had better each go and select good strong sticks for clubs, and we'll set to work at them."

When it grew dark we lighted our candle and, placing it in a holder, made of two crossing branches, inside the bower, we seated ourselves on our leafy beds and started to work. As Jack would only have time to make a bow and arrows for himself, Peterkin fashioned himself a spear and, using the coconut-tree cloth, I made myself a sling.

Before long, Peterkin had thinned down his spear and tied an iron point very cleverly to the end of it; I had formed a sling, the lines of which were composed of thin strips of the coconut cloth, plaited; and Jack had made a stout bow, nearly five feet long, with two arrows, feathered with two or three large plumes which a bird had dropped. The string of the bow was formed of our piece of whip-cord, part of which, as he did not like to cut it, was rolled round the bow.

Scarcely had the sun shone its first ray across the bosom of the broad Pacific next day, than Jack sprang to his feet,

and, hallooing in Peterkin's ear to awaken him, ran down the
beach to take his customary dip in the sea. We did not, as
was usual, bathe that morning in our Water Garden; but, in
order to save time, refreshed ourselves in the shallow water
just opposite the bower. Our breakfast was also dispatched
without loss of time, and, in less than an hour afterwards, all
our preparations for the journey were completed.

After walking along the shore for some time, we were
about to commence the exploration of a valley, when Peterkin
stopped us and directed our attention to a white column above
the rocks, as if of steam or spray. It rose upwards to a height
of several feet, and then disappeared.

In a few minutes we gained the spot, which was very rugged
and precipitous, and, moreover, quite damp with the falling
of the spray. While we stood there, anxiously waiting for the
reappearance of these waterspouts, we heard a low, rumbling

sound, which quickly increased to a gurgling and hissing noise, and a moment later a thick spout of water burst upwards from a hole in the rock, and spouted into the air with much violence, and so close to where Jack and I were standing that it nearly touched us. We sprang aside, but a cloud of spray descended, and drenched us both.

Peterkin, who was standing farther off, escaped with a few drops, and burst into an uncontrollable fit of laughter on beholding our miserable plight; but his merriment was put to a stop abruptly by the gurgling noise occurring close to where he stood.

"Where'll it spout this time, I wonder?" he said, looking about with some anxiety, and preparing to run. Suddenly there came a loud hiss or snort; a fierce spout of water burst up between Peterkin's legs, blew him off his feet, enveloped him in its spray, and hurled him to the ground.

It was now our turn to laugh, but we did not wait for

a further drenching. Lighting a fire some way off, we hung up our clothes to dry, and then walked down to the beach. We concluded that there must be a subterranean channel in the rock into which the water was driven by the larger waves, and finding no way of escape through these small holes, was thus forced up violently through them.

"I say, Ralph, what's that in the water? Is it a shark?" said Jack, just as we were about to quit the place.

I immediately ran to the overhanging ledge of rock, from which he was looking down into the sea, and bent over it. There I saw a very faint, pale object of a greenish colour, which seemed to move slightly while I looked at it.

"It's like a fish of some sort," said I.

"Hullo, Peterkin!" cried Jack. "Fetch your spear; here's work for it."

But when we tried to reach the object, the spear proved to

be too short. Jack now drove the spear forcibly towards the object, and let go his hold; but although it seemed to be well aimed, he must have missed, for the handle soon rose again; and when the spear was drawn up, there was the pale green object in exactly the same spot, slowly moving its tail.

Resolving to pay a visit to it again, at some more convenient season, we now set off once more on our travels. During the next two days, we made a complete circuit of Coral Island and came across many wonderful trees and plants, besides a lovely blue lake inhabited by ducks and water-fowl.

At another point, along the coast, we observed a cluster of little islands on one of which we could see a whole host of penguins. Jack told us that he planned to build a boat, so that we could pay penguin island a visit, as soon as we completed our excursion.

Peterkin succeeded in spearing a wild pig, and our supper on the night we spent away from home was a splendid meal. There was, first of all, the little pig; then there were taro-root, yam, potato, six plums, sugar-cane, and a wood-pigeon which I had killed with a stone from my sling.

On our homeward journey, we found the crumbling remains of a human habitation containing the skeletons of a man and his dog, and we wondered sadly who the unfortunate castaway had been. His hut had little in it, but we discovered an iron pot, a pistol and an old axe, all of which we brought away with us. Nearby, we came across a tame cat; this poor animal, which was almost blind and very deaf, was overjoyed at our arrival, so Peterkin picked it up and bore it back to our camp in his arms.

Late that evening, very tired, we reached our bower, where we found everything just as we had left it.

"Come, Jack," cried Peterkin, one morning about three weeks after our return from the long excursion, "let's be jolly today, and do something vigorous. I'm quite tired of hammering, hewing and screwing at that little boat of ours. Let us go on an excursion to the mountain-top, or have a hunt after the wild ducks, or make a dash at the pigs."

"We have not yet discovered the nature of the curious

object that we saw near the waterspouts," said I. "Shall we go over there?"

"Good idea, Ralph, let us away to the waterspouts!" cried Jack, going up to the bower for his bow and arrows. "And bring your spear, Peterkin. It may be useful."

On arriving at the waterspout rocks, we hastened down to the edge and observed the pale-green object still distinctly visible, moving its tail slowly to and fro in the water.

Peterkin immediately took the spear and darted it like an arrow into the sea. It went straight into the centre of the green object, passed quite through it, and rose immediately afterwards, pure and unsullied, while the tail moved quietly as before!

"Now," said Peterkin gravely, "that brute is a heartless monster; I'll have nothing more to do with it."

"I'm pretty sure," said Jack, "that it is merely a kind of phosphoric light."

"Well," said I, "there is nothing to hinder us from diving down to it, now that we are sure it is not a shark."

"True," returned Jack, stripping off his clothes; "I'll go down, Ralph, as I'm better at diving than you are." Jack stepped forward, joined his hands above his head, bent over the rocks, and plunged into the sea. When the water became still, we saw him swimming far down in the midst of the green object. Suddenly he sank below it, and vanished altogether from our sight! We gazed anxiously down at the spot where he had disappeared. Two minutes passed! Peterkin and I became more and more alarmed. I was just about to dive in after Jack, when his head rose to the surface.

"Jack!" we both cried. "Where were you? What kept you so long?"

Jack launched into his explanation: "Now, lads," said he, "that green object is a stream of light issuing from a cave in the rocks. I dashed into it, darted upwards, and found my head out of water. At first I could scarcely see anything as I gazed around me, it was so dark; but gradually my eyes became accustomed to it, and I found that I was in a huge cave, part of the walls of which I observed on each side of me. While I was looking around me, it came into my head that you two would think I was drowned; so I plunged down through the passage again, rose to the surface, and—here I am!"

I could not rest satisfied till I had dived down to see the cave. When I returned, we had a long conversation about it, and decided to explore the cave together, taking with us some highly inflammable bark, protected from the water by coconut cloth, which we could use as a torch.

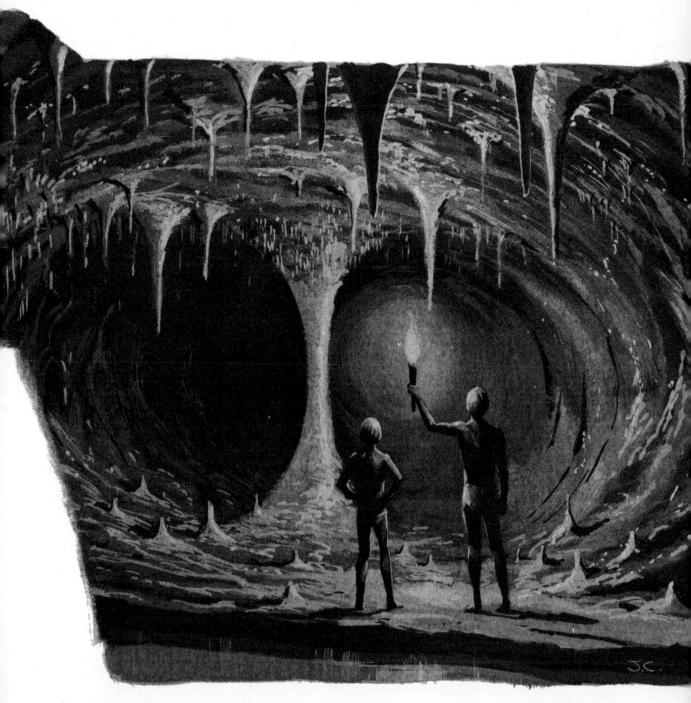

Poor Peterkin, being a non-swimmer, was too terrified of the water to accompany us, so Jack and I left him ashore and plunged into the sea.

Inside the cave, we landed on a shelving rock and, having succeeded in lighting the torch, found ourselves in a vast cavern made of coral with a limestone floor.

Before returning to Peterkin, we extinguished the torch and left it in a dry spot, in case we should have need of it on a future occasion.

The happy days on Coral Island flew by, with more than enough to occupy our time. When the boat was ready, we spent many hours afloat and paid a visit to the island of penguins, a voyage which nearly ended in disaster, because of a violent storm which suddenly blew up. Luckily, we found shelter on a rocky islet, and were able to return home when the tempest had blown itself out.

One day, however, our peaceful life was interrupted by the arrival of two native war-canoes. Aware of our danger, if we should be caught by savages, the three of us armed ourselves with clubs and hid behind a rock, round which we could keep watch on the fast-approaching canoes.

We now observed that the foremost canoe, which contained a few women and children as well as men, was being chased by the other, entirely filled with men.

When the leading canoe reached the shore, the women and children rushed into the woods, while the men prepared to resist the landing of their enemies. The fierce battle that ensued,

39

immediately the attacking party's canoe struck the beach, was frightful to behold. At last the first arrivals were overpowered, whereupon all the fifteen survivors were bound and carried into the woods.

The victorious savages kindled a fire of brushwood on the beach, whilst others rounded up the women and children from their refuge among the trees. Then a captive was dragged back on to the beach and clubbed to death, after which his executioners cut some slices of flesh from the man's body, roasted them over the fire and ate them.

We were naturally horrified to see all this, and when the giant leader of the victorious savages began to threaten the youngest of the three women — a modest, gentle-looking girl of a different race to the others — we could stand inaction no longer.

Leaving Peterkin and me to release the prisoners from their bonds, Jack uttered a frightful yell and leaped down upon the savages, who were at first too surprised to defend themselves from the blows which Jack rained on them with his whirling staff.

The chief, however, was very powerful, and it was only the arrival of Peterkin and myself, at the head of the released prisoners, that saved Jack from a quick death and finally overpowered the savages.

After the battle was over, we shook hands with all those whom we had saved and, although we were unable to converse, established friendly relations with them, discovering that the chief was named Tararo and the girl called Avatea.

The savages spent the night with us, after enjoying all the food that we could provide, and then prepared for the return journey to their distant island.

Tararo and his people rubbed noses with us in farewell,

carried their bound enemies aboard the canoes, stowed away some provisions, and left us alone again on Coral Island.

Not long after our adventure with the savages, a fresh intruder appeared over the horizon — a schooner flying the skull and crossbones!

Realizing that we must have been seen by the crew, who lowered a boat with the intention of landing as soon as the schooner had rounded to, close to the reef, we decided that our only chance of safety lay in the underwater cave.

At first, Peterkin implored us to leave him to chance his luck, so frightened was he at the thought of having to dive into the sea in order to enter the cave; but at last Jack and I persuaded him that, between us, we could carry him safely through the water into the cavern.

Peterkin behaved with great courage. He floated between us like a log of wood, and we passed the tunnel and rose into the cave without any trouble.

Jack lit the torch that was always kept in the cave, and we then discussed our situation. We decided to spend the night in the cave, hoping that the pirates would soon tire of looking for us and leave the island. Our emergency store of food was enough for our immediate needs, and some coconut cloth provided reasonable bedding.

Next morning, it was agreed that I should slip out of the cave and see what the pirates were about.

All was quiet when I bobbed up to the surface, so I crept slowly out of the water and up on to the cliff.

Looking out to sea, I saw the schooner sailing away, and uttered a shout of joy.

"There she goes!" I said aloud to myself. "The villains have been balked of their prey this time at least."

"Not so sure of that!" said a deep voice at my side, while at the same moment a heavy hand grasped my shoulder, and held it as if in a vice.

I had been tricked, and was now in the grip of the pirate captain. Tightening his grasp on my shoulder, he uttered a shrill whistle. At this signal, a party of his seamen soon came

into view, rowing the ship's boat round a nearby point which had hidden them from view.

The captain ordered me to light a fire, so that the smoke from it would warn the schooner that she should return to the island.

"Where are the other cubs?" the captain demanded to know.

"If you mean my companions," said I, "I won't tell you."

He drew a pistol from his belt, cocked it and said: "If you don't tell me all you know, I'll blow your brains out!"

"Villain!" said I. "You can do as you wish with me, but I shall tell you nothing!"

Although the captain was furious at being so defied, he did no worse than order me to be thrown into the boat, which was then rowed out to the schooner.

I was ordered aboard, and the ship put to sea again.

The captain soon sent for me and, apparently impressed by my refusal to give way to his threats, adopted a much more reasonable attitude.

When he had heard the story of our shipwreck on Coral Island, the captain explained that he was not really a pirate but a sandal-wood trader, and that he had to act ruthlessly because of the dangers to be overcome, on land and sea, when trading among the South Sea islands.

Seeing that I had no real option, I agreed to join the crew as his private cabin-boy; but, despite the captain's explanations, I still felt far from happy about him and his crew.

For many miserable weeks we sailed across the great sweep of island-scattered ocean, and all the time I grew increasingly anxious to escape from the schooner. The only member of the crew to whom I wished to speak, and who showed a scrap of human decency, was a sailor called Bill and, gradually, the two of us struck up a kind of friendship.

At last, we reached the island of Ema, where the captain intended to take on a cargo of sandal-wood. Although the principal chief, Romata, was suspicious of our intentions, owing to the cheating and bad behaviour he had endured on a previous occasion, he agreed to the proposed terms and we went ashore to commence cutting sandal-wood.

Romata was entertaining a visiting chieftain, and suggested that we should all watch a grand surf-swimming match which was to be held in honour of his guest.

One of the surf-swimmers came in on the crest of a wave most manfully, and landed almost on the spot where Bill and I stood. To my amazement, I recognized the features of Tararo. At the same moment, he recognized me and, advancing quickly, rubbed noses in greeting.

I explained to Bill how we had met before and, seeing that he understood the native language of those parts, asked him to inquire after Avatea.

Bill spoke to Tararo for some time, and then translated the information that he had obtained.

"Tararo is the chief who has been visiting Romata," he

explained, "and Avatea is a Samoan girl, who was captured in war and has since been brought up as Tararo's daughter. Your friend here is angry with her, however, because she won't marry the man he has chosen as her husband. It appears that she is engaged to a young chief whom Tararo hates, and he has threatened to kill her if, on his return home, she has not decided to do as he wishes."

I was shocked to hear this, and by much else that I heard and saw of the brutal practices of the heathen savages on Ema. But something even more disturbing occurred, aboard the schooner, a couple of days later.

Through an open skylight, I overheard the captain and the mate planning to outdo the native chief by creeping up on his village, attacking its inhabitants, and then, after seizing the rest of the cut sandal-wood, sailing away with their loot.

When I told Bill about this dastardly scheme, he agreed to help me thwart the plotters.

"I'll tell you what I'll do, Ralph," he said. "I'll swim ashore after dark and fix a musket to a tree, not far from the place where we'll have to land. Then I'll tie a long string to the trigger, so that, when our fellows cross it, they'll let it off, and so alarm the village in time to prevent an attack, but not in time to prevent us getting back to the boat."

This plan Bill duly carried out before, at midnight, the men were mustered on deck for the surprise attack. Using muffled oars, the schooner was rowed into a secluded creek, and then we all went ashore in the ship's boat, which I was left to guard while the men carried out the captain's orders.

My heart sank when, a few moments later, a faint click made it clear to me that Bill's priming had not caught, and thus our scheme to warn the savages had failed.

I waited alone in the dark by the boat until, suddenly, a single shot rang out. Then I heard yells of alarm from the village, followed by our captain cursing the man who fired the premature shot. After that, wild sounds of battle were borne to me. A few minutes later, I saw a large number of natives moving swiftly

47

through the woods towards the scene of battle, and realized that this was an outflanking force which would take our crew in the rear.

Sure enough this is how it turned out, and I soon heard the death-cries of the sailors, as they were overpowered by the savages.

What was I to do now? The only course of action open to me was to attempt escape in the schooner, although sailing her single-handed offered but a poor chance of success.

As I prepared to leave the shore in the ship's boat, Bill burst through the bushes and leapt aboard. We gained the schooner, cut the line of the anchor, manned the giant oars and glided away down the creek.

At that moment, the savages reached the bank of the creek, but too late to catch up with us, for the vessel was now moving rapidly out to sea.

When all was safely under control, and the schooner heading for Coral Island, I was shocked to find that poor Bill had been badly wounded ashore, the captain having deliberately shot him for firing the premature warning that I had heard.

I did my best to care for Bill, but he rapidly grew worse, and I was forced to leave him on the couch whilst I attended to the ship, for a violent squall broke upon us and I did not dare leave the tiller for even a second.

When the squall had passed, I was horrified to find that my only companion was dead, and that my own life now depended on my ability to handle the schooner, night and day, in all weathers, without assistance.

Somehow, I succeeded in this difficult task, largely due to calm seas, and everything went quite well, until early one morning I was overjoyed to see the familiar outline of Coral Island on the horizon.

I steered the schooner safely into the lagoon, let go the anchor and announced my arrival by firing the schooner's gun.

This was a most effective way of rousing Peterkin and Jack from their slumbers. They bounded from the bower, terrified by the bang and convinced that the pirates had returned.

"Hullo!" I shouted. "Peterkin! Jack! It's me!" After our happy reunion, I recounted all my adventures, and Jack described the difficulty he had had in bringing Peterkin out from the under-water cave after my disappearance.

"And now," continued Jack, "as we have a fine schooner at our disposal, I suggest that we visit some other islands of the South Seas, and shape our course for the island on which Avatea lives. Tararo should be grateful to us, and we may, therefore, be able to persuade him to allow the poor girl to marry the man to whom she is engaged."

Peterkin and I both thought this was a wonderful idea; so, having stocked up the schooner with plenty of food, we set sail for the island of Mango, where we were welcomed by the native teacher of a community of the islanders who had embraced Christianity.

Our new-found friend told us that Avatea was still on the island, living among the heathen people of whom Tararo was the chief. Moreover, we learnt that both the captive Samoan girl and the man she wished to marry were believers in the Christian faith.

The good teacher agreed to help in our attempt to secure Avatea's release by Tararo, although he warned us of the terrible dangers involved.

We sailed round the island to the heathen village and were greeted on the shore by Tararo. Through the Christian teacher, who acted as interpreter, he expressed much pleasure in seeing us, and asked what we wished to say to him.

The teacher explained that we came to beg that Avatea might be spared and allowed to follow her own wishes.

"What is his answer?" inquired Jack.

"I regret to say that he will not listen to the proposal. He says he has pledged his word to his friend that the girl shall be sent to him, and a deputy is even now on the island awaiting the fulfilment of the pledge."

At this moment a couple of men appeared, leading Avatea between them.

"Oh, my dear young friend," whispered the teacher, "she is to be sent away even now!"

"Is she?" cried Jack, dashing over two natives who stood in his way and seizing Avatea by the arm.

"Villain!" exclaimed Jack passionately. "I may die, but assuredly I shall not perish alone. I will not submit until you promise that this girl shall not be injured."

"You are very bold," replied Tararo haughtily, "but very foolish. Yet I will say that Avatea shall not be sent away, at least for three days."

"You had better accept Tararo's terms, Jack," said the teacher. "If you persist in this mad defiance, you will be slain and Avatea will be lost. Three days are worth having."

Jack hesitated a moment, and then reluctantly agreed.

The teacher whispered a few hasty words to Avatea; then Tararo advanced and led her unresistingly away, while Jack, Peterkin and I returned with the teacher to the schooner.

There, the teacher told us that he had a plan for saving Avatea, if we were prepared to run the risks attached to it.

Avatea had agreed, during his whispered conversation with her, to creep out to a quiet place on shore where we would be waiting in a canoe, well stocked with food, to escape with her to the island ruled by the man she loved.

The three of us readily agreed to make the attempt, and everything went according to plan.

Throughout the hours of darkness, and the whole of the following day, we plied our paddles. Then, that night, we were forced by utter weariness to stop for a meal and a few hours' sleep.

A thrilling cry of alarm from Peterkin awakened us sharply in the morning.

"What's wrong?" cried Jack, starting up.

Peterkin replied by pointing towards the horizon; and a glance was enough to show us that a large war-canoe was approaching at high speed!

The four of us paddled for all we were worth, and for sometime the war-canoe failed to reduce our lead.

Eventually, however, our strength began to ebb away and the pursuers crept up on us. Soon we gave up all hope of escape, and prepared to defend ourselves to the last with the paddles. But before any of us could strike a blow, the sharp prow of the war-canoe struck like a thunderbolt and hurled us into the sea.

When we recovered our senses, Peterkin, Jack and I were lying, bound hand and foot, in the bottom of the war-canoe.

On reaching Mango, we were hauled before Tararo, beside

whom stood the Christian teacher, with a look of anxiety on his mild features.

"How comes it," asked Tararo, turning to the teacher, "that these youths have abused our hospitality?"

"Tell him," replied Jack, "that we have not abused his hospitality, for his hospitality has never been extended to us. If I get another chance, I'll try to save Avatea yet!"

On hearing Jack's speech, Tararo frowned and his eyes flashed with anger.

"Go!" he said. "My debt to you is cancelled. You and your companions shall die!"

Immediately, we were seized, dragged away and thrust into a natural cave in a cliff; the entrance was then barricaded, and we were left alone in total darkness.

Only a fearful hurricane, that burst upon the island of Mango very soon after our imprisonment, saved us from a horrible death, without delay, at the heathens' temple of human sacrifice. The violence of the storm, however, was so great that the village was well nigh torn to pieces, and the savages fully occupied in saving both themselves and their property from destruction.

For a long, long month we remained in our dark and dreary prison, visited only by the silent savage who brought out daily food.

There have been one or two seasons in my life when I have felt as if the darkness of sorrow and desolation crushing my inmost heart could never pass away until death should make me cease to feel. The present was such a season.

One day, as we sat miserable and despairing in our prison, the jailer entered and advanced towards us with a knife in his hand. Going up to Jack, he cut the thongs that bound his wrists; then he did the same to Peterkin and me.

Surprised and uncertain, we waited to see if our captors intended to drag us to the temple for execution, but the jailer merely pointed to the cave's mouth, so we marched out into the open air.

There, the Christian teacher awaited us.

"Oh, my dear young friends," he cried, "through the great goodness of God you are free!"

"Free?" we cried together, in bewilderment.

"Ay, free," repeated the teacher, shaking us warmly by the hands. "A missionary has been sent to us, and Tararo has been persuaded to embrace the Christian religion!"

"And what of Avatea?" inquired Jack.

The teacher assured us that she had Tararo's permission to marry the Christian chief to whom she was engaged, and that he had already arrived for the wedding ceremony.

It was a bright, clear morning when we hoisted the snow-white sails of the schooner and left the shores of Mango, bound for Tahiti on the first stage of our journey home.

The teacher, the newly-arrived missionary, Tararo and his people, and Avatea and her husband, all came to bid us farewell and godspeed.

A thrill of joy, strangely mixed with sadness, passed through our hearts, as the retreating coastline signalled the end of our adventures among the green coral islands of the Pacific Ocean.